salt.

ISBN 10: 1492238287
ISBN-13: 978-1492238287

it was only and ever love.

for us

iyo. nchele. sira. muói. lonu. pa'akai. cho. masima. ama.
wardan. ityuwa. noon. salila. munya. zede´. chewa. mith.
nnu. lobon. hapi. letswai. juky. milh. sogum. mongwa.
uppu. saahl. cusbo. îunkyre. tisnt. lun. nkyen. ambel.
namak. gishiri. asin. chumvi. sohgoom. iam. malga. yim.
loon. mungwa. shio. uyah. zhiiwitaagan. îukyra. gleua.
isawudo. ta'ab. labana. meleh. ntsev. hoh-rum. aymara.
nkyini. yán. tswayi. sotoe. nun. chumbí. garam. disel.
nkyene. lu-nu. melh. tsira. nimak. sogidda. iztapinolli.
loonh. muño. umuchene. mithu. kashi. nkyene. melach.
lon. agh. krip. alati. tuz. sél. marili. suola. sol. sare. súl. só.
sil. halen. zout. salann. druska. salz. so. sale. sel. sal. salt.

salt.

water
clings to my
wrists.
it has been
my fragrance
since birth.

i am always writing.
of you.
for you.

— breath | my people

salt.

can we speak in flowers.
it will be easier for me to understand.

— other language

the morning is younger than you.
but
you will always be more tender.

— age

salt.

you broke the ocean in
half to be here.
only to meet nothing that wants you.

— immigrant

cruel mothers are still mothers.
they make us wars.
they make us revolution.
they teach us the truth. early.
mothers are humans. who
sometimes give birth to their pain. instead of
children.

— hate

salt.

sometimes
there is more water
in a poem
than in the sea.

———————————

three waves
wash their way
into my hand.
they are the water in this poem.

what
massacre
happens to my son
between
him
living within my skin.
drinking my cells.
my water.
my organs.
and
his soft psyche turning cruel.
does he not remember
he
is half woman.

— from

salt.

the hard season
will
split you through.
do not worry.
you will bleed water.
do not worry.
this is grief.
your face will fall out and down your skin
and
there will be scorching.
but do not worry.
keep speaking the years from their hiding places.
keep coughing up smoke from all the deaths you
have died.
keep the rage tender.
because the soft season will come.
it will come.
loud.
ready.
gulping.
both hands in your chest.
up all night.
up all of the nights.
to drink all damage into love.

— therapy

trust your work.

would
you still want to travel to
that
country
if
you could not take a camera with you.

— a question of appropriation

flower work
is
not easy.
remaining
soft in fire
takes
time.

salt.

when your mother unbirths you
because
she smells swans in your skin.
it feels like
she is
singing in salt.
and
her eyes carve you out of her body.
you
are a dream
undreamt.
and
this is a holocaust
that
winter birds
will
never know.

— swans

black women breathe flowers, too.
just because
we are taught to grow them in the lining of our
quiet (our grandmothers secret).
does not mean
we do not swelter with wild tenderness.
we soft swim.
we petal.
we scent limbs.
love.
we just have been too long a garden for sharp
and deadly teeth.
so we
have
grown
ourselves
into
greenhouses.

— greenhouses

i knew you.
before
i met you.
i've known you my whole life.

— nafsi

she asked
'you are in love
what does love look like'
to which i replied
'like everything i've ever lost
come back to me.'

salt.

when you are
here.
everything
is
wild.

— moon

are your eyes blushing ?

even the small poems mean something. they are
often whales in the bodies of tiny fish.

there
are
feelings.
you haven't felt yet.
give them time.
they are almost here.

— fresh

salt.

his back
was a hundred stories
he
wanted to tell me.
a hundred lives
he
wanted to live together.

— muscle (how many hours i spent reading his
skin)

i am such
a
sensitive summer thing.

when you are struggling
in your
writing (art).
it usually means
you
are hearing one thing.
but
writing (creating) another.

— honest | risk

i found flaws
and
they were beautiful.

— ugly

salt.

take the art.
slice it from their skin.
leave the color behind.

— flower crowns and bob marley t-shirts

my heart is in my mind. i think this is why i am
an artist.

i bleed
every month.
but
do not die.
how am i
not
magic.

— the lie

i will crawl for white beauty.
eat my arms.
barter my legs (make my thighs into altars of
grief).
for
skin that does not drink night.
hair that is not angry.
body that is not soil.
i place curses on my flesh
call them diets.
tell my ancestors
they are ugly.
howl at my nose until it bleeds.
run my heart across my teeth, repeatedly.
i am dying.
to be
beautiful.
but
beautiful.
is
something.
i
will never
be.

— by the time we are seven

salt.

where
you are.
is not
who
you are.

— circumstances

i am a child of three countries.
the water.
the heat.
the words.

salt.

lay down.
let me put your flowers on.

— fall

both.
i want to stay.
i want to leave.
i am three oceans away from my soul.

— lost

i lied.
i told you i was not afraid to love you.
then i walked away.
and
loved you.

— i have spent my whole life alone. loving you.
| when we choose fear

i am your friend.
a soul for your soul.
a place for your life.
home.
know this.
sun or water.
here
or
away.
we are a lighthouse.
we leave.
and
we stay.

— lighthouse

salt.

she was the color of evening husk
and salt.
i wore my voice with her sometimes.
my fragrance
others.
she was a beautiful place to bare my legs.
night my countries.
and
eat the hot winter.

— thaw

if i write
what you may feel
but cannot say.
it does not
make
me a poet.
it makes me a bridge.
and
i am humbled
and
i am grateful
to assist your heart in speaking.

— grateful

salt.

expect sadness
like
you expect rain.
both
cleanse you.

— natural

african american women are easy. inferior.
africans are dirty. jungle people.
african americans are lazy. indolent.
african people are too black. ugly.
african americans think they are better than us.
africans think they are better us.

— listen to the sound of us | we are breaking
our mothers heart | the ancestors weep at how
much we look like the hate that came to eat us

salt.

sit in the ocean.
it is one of the best medicines
on the planet.

— the water

if we must
both
be right.
we will
lose
each other.

— exile

he was so beautiful
because
when he held her
he was not concerned with 'being a man.'
'being a man'
had nothing to do with this.
these flowers pouring from his chest.

— weight

we are never our own.
we must change this fact.

— acceptance

salt.

i wake
to you everywhere.
yet
you are not here.

— reach

my english is broken.
on purpose.
you
have to try harder to understand
me.
breaking this language
you so love
is my pleasure.
in your arrogance
you presume that i want your skinny language.
that my mouth is building a room for
it
in the back of my throat.
it is not.

— i have seven different words for love. you
have only one. that makes a lot of sense.

salt.

i don't pay attention to the
world ending.
it has ended for me
many times
and began again in the morning.

the idea of a second heart.

i want more 'men'
with flowers falling from their skin.
more water in their eyes.
more tremble in their bodies.
more women in their hearts
than
on their hands.
more softness in their height.
more honesty in their voice.
more wonder.
more humility in their feet.

— less

you tell me
'burn yourself white, it will make me happy.'
my sadness
is sharpening itself against my teeth.
you are the color of soft coal.
and
just got back from visiting your mother in
nigeria last month.
you say 'look baby, look, what i brought back
for you.'
i move out.
.

lunch with your sister is slightly trembling.
you want to touch her opening cheek with your
hurt.
she won't really look at you.
it is better not to talk.
no words can put out the pale fire spreading
across her face.

salt.

.
you are sore from all of the white women in
magazines.
coaxing you out of your skin.
their fragrance is all over your friends
at school.
you can smell it.
the heat of whiteness on their necks.
'maybe,'
as your hands.
brush pain and relief into your face.
'maybe, now'
you say,
'the world will leave me alone.'

— bleach

if your light falls out of your mouth
pick it up.
(and
put it back).

— noor

salt.

you
will drown
if
you do not have boundaries.
they
are
not optional.
this structure
counts
on your inability
to
say
no.
mean no.
they take no
from
our
first breath.
go back
and
return it to your mouth.
your heart.
your light.

— swim | women of color

you
see your face.
you
see a flaw.
how. if you are the only one who has this face.

— the beauty construct

white people are not chinese.
because they are born/live in china.
white people are not indian.
because they are born/live in india.
white people are not african.
because they are born/live on a continent they
murdered their way into.

— there is no such thing as a white african |
colonial blood myths | a revisionist history

i am often broken into language.
whether i want to
speak or not.

salt.

i am simply the poet.
the
poem
is
the one
that
can change your life.

— medium

is there a place in the
community.
for
those who leave.
but
never leave (you).

— ex

salt.

i am the line.
on both sides there are songs
in my name.

— bi

the rain in this room
is low and thick
and
undressing my heart
through the air.

— intimacy

salt.

stay soft. it looks beautiful on you.

nayyirah waheed

i could just simply say
i want you.
and
leave my mouth in your hand.

salt.

we lay
in our country.
love makes us a homeland.

— bed

i am a brutally soft woman.

salt.

with
the water bowl balancing
on my thighs.
i soak the flowers.
until
they become words.
then i write.

— ritual

she washes the sea
on her knees.

— salt

salt.

i am a black wave
in
a white sea.
always seen
and
unseen.

— the difference

what will your eyes do with me
when they are done.
will they lay me
in the tender flesh behind
the sun.
fold me into
your memory's back.
keep me
a
running
water down your arms.

— where

salt.

stay is a sensitive word.
we wear
who stayed
and
who left
in our skin forever.

— sojourn

what
we hide
and do not
say
turns into
another mouth
that
only we know.

— mouths

salt.

as a woman
i know the difference between
appreciation
and
teeth.
what really hurts
is that
as a girl
i had to know the same thing.

— survivor

i am a silk field of vulnerability.

be careful
of all the things
you lose
in someone's mouth
when you love them.

if you deserve
honey
mine will flow from my arms to yours
no effort, no asking.
but, if there is none
and
you feel wind instead.
know
that my spirit already
senses that
when you smell sweetness
you
begin harvesting blades in your hands.

— kindness is a form of intelligence

salt.

what can i do
when the night comes
and
i break into stars.

— osmosis

do not
put
your hand
in the mouth of loneliness.
its teeth are soft
but it will scar you for life.

— do not be seduced by the lonely ones

salt.

you travel
to lush looted countries.
parts of earth laying on their sides.
barely breathing.
hot with rust, infection, and tourist anemia.
you and your camera arrive.
start tearing at bodies
with
your lust.
it's harmless.
appreciating culture.
sharing.
honoring clothing.
the way certain skin exists.

oh
you've sold those photographs.
the ones you were so excited about.
the one you 'caught' with children being
children.
the one with the woman you thought so
'beautiful'.
you and your camera
eat
as much as one stomach and three sd cards can
hold.
get on a plane
and
leave with the belief
that
your eyes are
clean.
honest.
artistic.

— photography | the gaze

salt.

the night was busy making the moon
so
i gathered my quilt
and softly
told my heart
we'd come back
tomorrow.

my whole life
i have
ate my tongue.
ate my tongue.
ate my tongue.
i am so full of my tongue
you would think speaking is easy.
but it is not.

— for we who keep our lives in our mouths

africa does not need your tears.
or
your prayers.
or
your money.
or
your t-shirts.
or
your telethons.
or
your hands ever so lovingly placed
on her buttocks.
your mouth at her breasts.
your fists in her eyes.
she wants you to stop pissing in her face
and
calling it water.

she wants you to leave.
she is the mother.
she does not belong to you.
you do not belong to her.
and
you hate this.
but
one day
you will reap.
what
you have sown.

— aid

men give birth, too.
to children.
to longings.
to dreams.
that they must hide.
their stomachs.
their uteruses.
their hungers.
their softness.
their cravings for touch.
to be
a
man.
is the thing
that closes their light.
and
eats their eyes.

— him

there is you and you.
this is a relationship.
this is the most important relationship.

— home

cry wild.
you have probably never cried wild.
but, you know what doors
feel like.
you have
an intimacy with doors
that is killing you.

— break

decolonization
requires
acknowledging.
that your
needs and desires
should
never
come at the expense of another's
life energy.
it is being honest
that
you have been spoiled
by a machine
that
is not feeding you freedom
but
feeding
you
the milk of pain.

— the release

salt.

why can we never
talk
about the blood.
the blood of our ancestors.
the blood of our history.
the blood between our legs.

— blood

i will tell you, my daughter
of your worth
not your beauty
every day. (your beauty is a given. every being is
born beautiful).
knowing your worth
can save your life.
raising you on beauty alone
you will be starved.
you will be raw.
you will be weak.
an easy stomach.
always in need of someone telling you how
beautiful you are.

— emotional nutrition

salt.

good + girl.

— rope

your heart is the softest place on earth. take care
of it.

the
diaspora is absolutely breathtaking.
and
the diaspora is in stunning pain.
we
are
a great many things. all at once.

— myriad | disconnect

getting yourself together.
what about undoing yourself.

— the fix

thick compassion.
as thick as the throats of our fathers
when they have already left
but leave their words behind.

.

our fathers write us. all over us. their
handwriting. we cannot ignore. whether they
have spelled our eyes. our mouths. or the need
in our brows. we cannot help but be their poem.

.

how could they think they are not important. we
are houses eaten by rivers because we do not
know their smell. when we are looking all the
way through ourselves, we are looking for them.
how dare they remove themselves from our
sight. we have a right to be able to recognize our
father if he is passing us on the street.

.

what kind of heart break is he. what night was it
that he decided. what did the moon look like.
was he hungry. so hungry, that he would give me
up. give us up. how do they give us up so easily.
so willingly. they take out their voice. break us
from it. and eat mist and guilt until we are but
dreams.

unharm someone
by
telling the truth you could not face
when you
struck instead of tended.

— put the fire out (unburn)

the beauty of my people
is
so
thick and intricate.
i spend days
trying
to undo my eyes
so
i can sleep.

— lace

if
the ocean
can calm itself
so can you.
we
are both
salt water
mixed
with
air.

— meditation

racism is a translucent skin.
it defends itself
by
attacking itself.

— reverse racism

in our own ways
we all break.
it is okay
to hold your heart outside of your body
for
days.
months.
years.
at a time.

— heal

you.
not wanting me.
was
the beginning of me
wanting myself.
thank you.

— the hurt

eyes that commit.
that is what I am looking for.

salt.

warm philadelphia night. blue bruise across the sky.
groceries in hand. i dreamt last night of honey. my
grandmother called me into a dream like she used to
call me into a room. she gave me honey. honey for
you. you, who will not talk. who will not swallow the
news. who will not let anything near your throat. but,
i can find you. i can find you even when you are
there, in morocco. even when you have flown
through your eyes but not your body. when you are
holding me, and i am practicing being limp with
restraint, because i am really holding you. when you
refuse to change back from water and want to fill our
whole house with the sebou. i know, my sweet. we
have talked about her the entire length of our love.
she was your eyes the day i met you. remember, you
and i. on the floor, you teaching me of how she eats.
three fingers on the right hand only. i have worn her
clothes. ate her language from your mouth. and i
knew, i knew when the phone calls came, and the tv
started shrieking, and our house turned into weather,
i knew this would break some of our bones. but my
love, it is drinking us down to our teeth. i cannot see
you anymore. your smile. your legs. your heat. is
lonely. the honey, grandmother said, is for your
blood. it is to bring you back. but, she said, i must
first ask, 'if' you want to come back. and though, 'if'
is razor to my vein, i will ask. so, i am not asking
'when' you will come back. because, i can take it, the
swimming in your body, the lostness, your growing
appetite for doors. i am not asking when. 'when,' is
not something you ask someone when the bodies of
their aunt. uncle. friends. first love. cannot be found.
i am asking, 'if.' because i am here. dangling from

your left ring finger, wringing oceans out of my skin,
and coming home every night. i know family is tattoo
and it is their screaming voices you hear when i say i
love you. i know, she is the love you are, the land you
are made of, and she is hemorrhaging. war is eating
her heart. but, my love, it is eating ours too.

— what the war has done to us

white people try to take
blackness.
pour it out
rub it into their skin
and
wear us
like they know what we about.
but
honey
it's only ever gon' be a suntan.
you
ain't neva gon' be black.

— tan | stealing from the sun

stop speaking.
use your eyes, instead.

— the eye fire

be insecure
in peace.
allow yourself
lowness.
know that it is
only
a
country
on
the way to who you are.

— traveling

if
we.
are
with child.
and
you believe that fatherhood
begins
when my body pours a baby into your hands.
not before.
you do not deserve this child.
you are a coward.

— you are a father the moment you enter me

do
not ever
be
afraid to tell me
who you are.
i am going to find
out
eventually.

— blunt

you ask
to touch my hair.
or worse
touch it without asking.
this is not innocence.
this is not ignorance.
this is not curiosity.
this is the very racist and subhuman belief
that
you have a right to me.

— i will break your hand | do not ever touch
me | every time you touch me. my ancestors
place a curse on you

your soul stained my shoulders.
my whole life smells like you.
this
will take time.
undoing you from my blood.

— the work

our ache
for
africa.
is
the heart
behind
our heart.
the pain with no name.

— amnesia

salt.

i am a woman
and
a poem.

— visceral

when you allow
that man.
to walk through your children.
plant his feet.
in
veins.
hold their voices.
necks.
bodies.
inside his violence.
you are no longer a mother.
when you give him the key to that door. because
you need to be loved by someone.
you have seasoned them for the wolf.
burned their childhood into fantasy.
it's going to take a third of their lives.
all the courage.
from
their cells to their hair.
to learn the alchemetic formula
that
turns that kind of betrayal.
a demothering.
soft.
liveable.

— before you get that key made

salt.

the worst
thing that ever happened
to
the world
was
the white man coming across gun powder.

— the end of the world | the beginning of
white supremacy

soon
the moon will come from my lips
and
you will not remember your name.

— oshún

salt.

there is a phantom language in my mouth.
a tongue beneath my tongue.
will i ever
remember what
i sound
like.
will i ever come home.

— african american i

i lost a whole continent.
a whole continent from my memory.
unlike all other hyphenated americans
my hyphen is made of blood. feces. bone.
when africa says hello
my mouth is a heartbreak.
because i have nothing in my tongue
to answer her.
i do not know how to say hello to my mother.

— african american ii

salt.

can you be a daughter.
if you have no
mother language.

— african american iii

how beautiful
that you can lay down a map
and with a straight finger
show me who you are.
you say
'show me, show me who you are.'
i tell my soft tight finger
'do not be afraid'
i slow and lightly
lay it on africa (as if i do not belong to her).
and
then
you ask me
'where.'

— african american iiii

salt.

we are afraid.
ashamed.
of
africa.

— the secret we never say | african american
iiiii

i like
the heat
in certain words.
the warm travel.
the low sun.

you do not have to be a fire
for
every mountain blocking you.
you could be a water
and
soft river your way to freedom
too.

— options

sometimes the night wakes in the
middle of me.
and i can do nothing
but
become the moon.

salt.

i want to see
brown and black folks
photographed
by
brown and black eyes.

— eyes

to not be safe on the earth.
simply
because
of the color of your skin.
how does a being survive this.

— trayvon martin

if
a man
can
only show vulnerability
for
what is between my legs.
can
only
be
a
heart
during
sex.
if an orgasm
is
the only way
he
can
weep.
what is his life
but
a cage.

— prison

listen to my poems.
but
do not look for me.
look for you.

— you

i am not yours.
i did not make the long hard journey through
and across the spirit world
to
be a man's ocean.
my body is not yours.
my mouth is not yours.
my water is not yours.
nothing i am belongs to you.
unless i decide
to
open my hand
and
give it to you.

— birthmarks

you will find your way.
it is
in the
same place
as
your love.

— seek

when
you tell yourself
'you can have your energy back.'
after years
of
giving
it
to white people.
and
their
requirements for acceptance. for supple
colonization.
digesting
their beliefs.
thoughts.
opinions.
of
you.

when you remove them from your nucleus.
your being is then
allowed
to
focus
its power
on
turning your life.
into.
your soul's work.
you become yours.
again.

— decolonization | center

to
call me
black.
is
one of the most beautiful.
incredible.
compliments
you could ever give me.

— insult

your skin
smells
like light.
i think you are
the
moon.

salt.

i broke myself
dreaming of you last night.
the
water and flowers
have been
working on me all morning.

— seamstresses

if you show
someone the sun in your bones
and they reject you
you must remember.
they hurt themselves this very same way.

— unable

'no'
might make them angry.
but
it will make you free.

— if no one has ever told you, your freedom is
more important than their anger

there is a tender thing
i am made of.
i have always felt before i breathe.

and what if i write of you.
is that more love than you can handle.

be a lion.
i will still be water.

where are my legs. where are my legs. i had to give them to my babies so they could swim back home to me. back home to me. back home to me. i rubbed the sun all in their hair. every single birth. i rubbed sun in their hair. so they remember who they look like. who they look like. who they look like. me. to lose love that way. to have to watch them be opened like that. all the way down to their mouths. time will never know my skin. wild with everything and nothing but them. i sang into their blood. each and every one of them have my voices in their bones. they will come home. i know they will come home. the whole sky had to hold me when the world came to eat my children. that fear. that pain. that fear. that pain. that fear. that pain. that fear. that pain. that fear. that pain. that fear. that pain. that fear. that pain. that fear. that pain. that fear. that pain. that fear. that pain. that fear. that pain. that fear. that pain. that fear. that pain. wake up my loves. into me. i will come to you every night. every single night. because you do not understand your nose. or your feet. or the boats in your eyes. you do not remember me. and you suffer. you suffer. you suffer. you suffer. you suffer. you suffer. you suffer. you suffer. swept with banzo. swept with banzo. swept with banzo. you suffer. you hate yourself. you hate me. this is death for a mother. how many deaths.

i am your mother. i am your mother. i am your mother. i am your mother. i am your mother. i am your mother. i am your mother. i am your mother. i am your mother. i am your mother. remember me. remember me. remember me. my hands in your heart. i won't let you go. i will find you. worlds away from me. i am your beauty. i am you. no matter how much bleach you must drink. every night i will come into you and repair. relove. undo everything that is not me. i memorized you. i will walk over all waters to come and get you. bring you back to me. they do not know. they do not know. they do not know. they do not know. they do not know. they do not know. they do not know. they do not know. they do not know. they do not know. they do not know. they do not know. they do not know. they do not know. they do not know. they do not know. they do not know i put salt in each one of your skin. each and every one of your skins. they do not know that salt preserves not only fruit. but children. you will remember. you will remember. you will remember. you will remember. you will remember. you will remember. you will remember. you will remember. you will remember. you see. my love. you see how your body is beginning to slow glow with stars. you are remembering. you are mine. you have never been anything else.   — africa's lament

salt.

these are not tears.
this is the sea.

— tides

never
trust anyone
who says
they do not see color.
this means
to them
you are invisible.

— is

when i am afraid to speak
is when i speak.
that is when it is most important.

— the freedom in fear

nayyirah waheed

what i never
learned
from my mother
was that
just because someone desires you
does not
mean
they value you.
desire is the kind of thing
that
eats you
and
leaves you starving.

— the color of low self esteem

being in love with my people
does
not mean i hate others.
how ridiculous is that.

— self

i am relieved.
when
i see the feminine presence
in a man's eyes.
it means
he is a peace
i do not
have
to
bring to him.

— ease

apologize to your body.
maybe
that's where the healing begins.

— starting

the most
gorgeous thing
on
a human being.
vulnerability.

— want

salt.

put
some salt in that honey.
warm it up.
heal.

— stove

a black woman
can write of
loneliness.
or
love
or softness.
or the moon.
you may try valiantly
to cripple her.
but she will still grow flowers in her flesh.

— a genocide of flowers

salt.

you blush like an ocean in love.
wild with blueness.

— yemanja

i have always been the woman of my dreams.

salt.

open
your eyes.
even if
the
sun wants them.

— see

audre wrote
of
the
'secret poetry.'
we all know
this
poetry.
lining our arms.
rusting our teeth.
walking through our hair.
feeding
our wild stomach.
soothing
our
mouth tears.
folding itself into waists.
between legs.
always
climbing up our sadness
into
our necks
to
sleep.

— the secret poetry | audre

there is peaceful.
there is wild.
i am both at the same time.

— sum

all that was
taken
from me
is still here.

— root | immortal

salt.

this
hard vulnerability.

— black

even if you are a small forest surviving off of
moon alone.
your light is extraordinary.

— reminder

a woman
is
not a girl.
and
a girl
is
not a woman.

— misogyny | synonyms

some people
when they hear
your story.
contract.
others
upon hearing
your story.
expand.
and
this is how
you
know.

you
are
my favorite kind.
nothing
that i can
name.

i lost my hands
in her waist
and
that is the softest detail.

consider this place.
consider this place
as safe.
when you take off your throat.
lay your voice in the middle of the bed.
open your back up to me.

— slow

if you are softer
than before
they came.
you
have been loved.

if someone
does not want me
it is not the end of the world.
but
if i do not want me.
the world is nothing but endings.

something as simple as
the
sun
asking me
out.

— the perfect date

salt.

my silence
is wet and hot
and
drinking my mouth to death.

you are not a mistake. you are too many
exquisite details to be a mistake.

salt.

1. rub honey into the night's back.
2. make sure the moon is fed.
3. bathe the ocean.
4. warm sing the trees.

— tend

nayyirah waheed

the warmest light is your body.

it is being honest
about
my pain
that makes me invincible.

— yield

when summer comes
the air runs hot with fever
and
so do i.

— alchemy

you took off your mouth.
gave it to him.
and
now
you secretly
weep fire
in the bathroom
before making love.
how much burning
will be
enough.

— dowry

your soul is inflamed.
good.
pay attention.
find water.
come inside.

— map

salt.

i am a dream still dreaming.

i do not expect my child's respect.
just because i have given birth to their life.
does not mean they owe me.
anything.
what i want most is to look into my child's eyes
and
see
that i have given birth
to
a
heart.
have
honored.
held and fed.
someone's heart.
from the moment we first met.
and they love me for this.

— first

there have been so many times
i have seen a man wanting to weep
but
instead
beat his heart until it was unconscious.

— masculine

you are a story.
do not become a word.
one word.
because you want to be loved.
love does not ask you to be nothing
for
something.

— name

i s t u,,,,,m b l e in this lan guage.
i fa ll down in this lang ua GE.
i am p & a & i & n = in this lang | uage.
my (mouth). heart. arms are losing muscle + in this l
a n g u age.
my body does not $ recognize the taste $ of this -
language-.
i long

---

in this LANGUAGE.
i am not/ {myself} in this l anguage."

— e.n.g.l.i.s.h./ for all of us who are held
captive

healing
begins
the moment
you
want it to.

— time

salt.

i touched her in the middle of her heart.
i never saw her again.

— scar

you
keep putting your hands
on my mind.
it is the same thing as my body.

— hands

salt.

leaving.
doesn't mean that
you've left.

— linger

my
mother
was
my first country.
the first place i ever lived.

— lands

salt.

eat stars.

— how to heal the native wounds | fire work

_____

eat water.

— how to heal the diasporic wounds |
salt work

for you, i am sweeping words against each other.

— quilts

salt.

go.
enjoy.
leave.
it was all about you, anyway.

— tourist

i do not want to be liked.
i want to be myself.

— fiction

salt.

your
skin
is infamous
for making me late to work.

— you know i ain't got time for that laugh and
those eyes. you ain't right.

nayyirah waheed

i am a quiet singer.

i do not feel
i need a name or a movement
to legitimize the defense of myself.
i am a woman of color.
my bones have been
bought and sold every morning.
so, now i carry a machete in my
mouth.

— ivory

i loved you
because
it was easier
than
loving myself.

— runaway

salt.

as a child
there was either
books
or
pain.
i chose books.

— how i became a writer

some words build houses in your throat. and
they live there. content and on fire.

you say
'you are such a 'good writer' for a woman of
color.'

i hear
'you have a better command of the english
language than i do.
my bitterness is wild salt in my blood
causing
my organs to crush and weep
and
this is the sound of my pain.'

— translation | white noise

remember.
you were a writer
before
you ever
put
word to paper.
just because you were not writing
externally.
does not mean you were not writing
internally.

— stories

illegitimate children
is such a foreign concept to me.
i was born from my mother
and
i am here.
that is
all the legitimacy i need.

— the bastard construct

knowing your power
is what creates
humility.
not knowing your power
is what creates
insecurity.

— ego

if we
wanted
to.
people of color
could
burn the world down.
for what
we
have experienced.
are experiencing.
but
we don't.

— how stunningly beautiful that our sacred
respect for the earth. for life. is deeper than
our rage

if i have never seen you cry.
if you do not cry.
if you do not value or respect the needs of your
water.
you and i cannot form.
if you cannot allow your own being
to wash over you.
how will mine ever make it past your skin.

— available

beautiful
is the highest compliment
you
can pay a woman.
i watch women
dive.
to the ground.
eat it.
stand up.
and
smile.

— shame

if you can not
hear
them.
ask the ancestors
to
speak louder.
they only whisper
so
as not to frighten you.
they know
they have been convinced.
coerced.
spooked.
from your skin.

— communication

weather
is the
earth's
emotions.
she is obviously
enraged.

— sentient

there
are some wounds.
only
africa
can
heal.

— in us

a lie
is
simply a lie.
it draws its strength from belief.
stop believing
in
what hurts you.

— power

your words walk down my back.
this is how
you leave me.

— vertebrae

will you always be this pain in me.
will you always hurt.

you must
put
healing on the list.
the grocery list.
the to do list.
the night list.
because
you are teaching
your
baby
the very same chemistry
that
took your eyes
and
heart when you were four.

— the list

you.
are
your
own
standard of
beauty.

— mirror work

make sure
they have fallen in love
with
your spirit.
first.
your body.
second.

— the fragrance of your laughter

i fell apart many times.
so.
what does that say about me
besides
i live through
wars.

my ancestors made sure
i was born
the color of their
eyes.

— sight

have you ever
heard
a black woman weep over her skinmurdered
child.
it is the splitting of atoms.
it is billions
of
voices screaming their children's names
through
her death wail.

— trayvon martin ii

nayyirah waheed

do you think
calling me 'angry'
is an insult.
every time you call me 'angry'
i hear your voice salt with guilt
and
i laugh.
look how easy it is to reveal you.

— anger is a healthy and natural response to
oppression

it's not about making you uncomfortable.
it's about making me comfortable.

— reparations

i think one
of the most pathological
things i have ever seen
is
stabbing
someone
and
then telling them that
their
pain and anger
over being stabbed
is
making you sad.

— white guilt

you can not
remain
a
war
between
what you want to say (who you really are).
and
what you should say (who you pretend to be).
your mouth was not designed to eat itself.

— split

chemistry
is
you touching my arm
and
it
setting fire to my mind.

— flood

you ask
your heart
why it is always hurting.
it says
'this is the only thing you will allow me to say to
you.
the only feeling you are willing to feel.'

weep.
into your shirt.
you're allowed.

— clouds

he said
'my absence is strong and warm.
it will hold
you.
it will teach you how to miss.
how to be without.
and
how to survive anyway.'

— how my father raised me

the stars
will begin falling
from your mouth.
the moment.
you forgive yourself.
for the silence.
you
did not create.

— fault

'i love myself.'
the
quietest.
simplest.
most
powerful.
revolution.
ever.

— ism

i want you
to
drink the sea inside of me.

— summer juice

salt.

i dropped my pride
in the gulf of your mouth.
and
i do not know how to swim.

— island

nayyirah waheed

i look for you
in the middle of the light.
in the west of the day.
in the warm memory of the water.

salt.

she is poem country.
everywhere
a
language.

writing.
is the way
your
being speaks to you.

— conversations

you are digging into my heart
with both of your hands.
who. what. are you looking for.
i am right here.

— trust

i wake up in a poem.

salt.

i knew
read
sonia sanchez.
nikki giovanni.
audre lorde.
before
i ever even
heard the name
charles bukowski.
finally,
a proper education.

— the order

hire her.
for your children.
for your kitchen.
for your clothes.
for your house.
give her a room
with an unmade twin bed and a dresser. an alarm
clock.
set her hours
past her own children's bed time.
shorten her name.
change her name.
talk through her.
call her a part of the family. without ever asking
if she wants you this close to her skin.
just
do not be surprised the day
you accidently
look in her eyes
and
her spirit pulls your heart out through your
mouth.

— the maid

who you are.
is not what you are doing.
what you are doing
is
being
someone else.

— architecture

her love.
was the only medicine.
the only
medicine.
that ever worked. and this is why
she left.
she
wanted yours to work. too.

— healer

salt.

the thing you are most
afraid to write.

write that.

— advice to young writers

nayyirah waheed

when i am lost
touch the back of my water
and
i will return.

the wounds have changed me.
i am so soft with scars
my skin
breathes and beats stars.

i have lost millions and millions
of words to fear.
tell me that is not violence.

— the deaths

if she is warm
let me
know her in the morning.

we write from the body.
it remembers everything.

— melanin| bone and soil

salt.

your
hands pouring sky
all over my
bed.
what language is that.

your mother may
never return from war.
but
you will still see her every day.

— two

salt.

fall apart.
please
just, fall apart.
open your mouth.
and
hurt. hurt the size of everything it is.

— dam

she was flower salt in my heart, and she hurt
beautifully.

for me
there is no other.
because there is no default.
everyone
is
a variation of life.

— the human being | the human gender | the
human sex

it was
i
who held you.
when
you
wanted
someone else.

—— treason

i saw love
there
i just did not pick it up.

— mistake

express your sadness.
inside
it has only one place to go.

— tissue

salt.

you are trailing long dust
across
our heart.
there is an easier way to leave.

— over

you.
the weight.
rose cinnamon.
dark honey.
the clothes you wear on your mouth.
the warm smoke in your legs.
a quiet quilt.
a mason jar (for moon).
an easy laugh brushed with oil.
time.
the light left over.
some music in your hair.
you.

— things you bring to the ocean at night

salt.

why is the moon
full.
is it carrying the whole world
too.

— daughter

you are a sea of light.
open your eyes.
see yourself.

i am terrified.
then i remember
i am
giving birth to a continent.
i remember
that
i am giving birth
to
a continent over and over.

— the process | writing a book | the ancestors
were my midwives | ashé.

67278659R00156

Made in the USA
Lexington, KY
07 September 2017